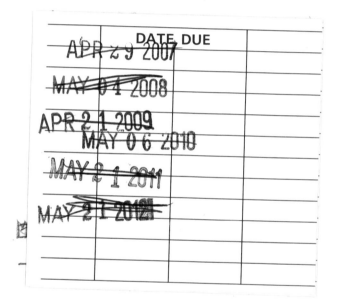

Celebrating
Earth Day

by Janet McDonnell
illustrated by Diana Magnuson

created by Wing Park Publishers

CHILDRENS PRESS®
CHICAGO

Library of Congress Cataloging-in-Publication Data

McDonnell, Janet, 1962-
    Celebrating Earth Day / by Janet McDonnell.
      p.   cm. — (Circle the year with holidays)
    Summary: Ms. Webster's class plans a party to celebrate Earth Day.
    ISBN 0-516-00689-4 (lib. bdg.)
    [1. Earth Day—Fiction.   2. Environmental protection—Fiction.
3. Parties—Fiction.]   I. Title   II. Series.
PZ7.M1547Ce   1994
[E]—dc20   93-37714
                                                   CIP
                                                   AC

Celebrating
Earth Day

It was the first warm day of spring, and Ms. Webster's class was restless. "Why do we have to be inside," complained Sara. "It's so warm and pretty outdoors."

"You're right," said Ms. Webster. "Follow me, everyone." The pupils looked at each other in shock. "Wow! We get to have class outside!"

"Under this big oak tree," said Ms. Webster. "This is the perfect place to talk about our plans."

"Plans for what?" asked Hector.

"Friday is April 22, Earth Day! On that day, we celebrate our beautiful planet."

5

"You mean we get to have a party?" asked Jeremy.

"Yes, but Earth Day means more than that," said Ms. Webster. "It reminds us to do what we can to take care of the earth. We need to help keep the water, air, and land clean."

"How can we take care of a whole planet? I can't even keep my room clean," said Allison.

"We can't do it by ourselves, but if we do our part, while people in other lands do their part, the earth will be a better place!"

The next day, Hector asked, "How do we start caring for the earth?"

"I'm glad you asked," said Ms. Webster as she gave everyone a pair of rubber gloves. "We start by cleaning up the bike path."

"Yuck! Look at all the junk. This is worse than my room," said Allison.

"Litter is not only ugly. It can be dangerous," said Ms. Webster. "Animals sometimes get stuck in the plastic rings that hold packs of soda. And broken glass can cut people and animals. So let's get ready for Earth Day by cleaning up the litter. Put any cans and paper you find in bags. Use the box for bottles. But leave the broken glass for me to clean up."

Soon Ms. Webster's class had picked up every piece of trash. "The path looks beautiful again," said Sara.

"Look at all the garbage we collected!" said Jeremy.

"The cans and bottles are not really garbage. They can be recycled!" said Ms. Webster. "That means they can be used again and again. The metal and glass will be melted down to make new cans and bottles. Some paper can be recycled too. So can some kinds of plastic."

"What about the other stuff?" asked Hector.

"That's a good question," said Ms. Webster. "Most people throw away their garbage and never think about it again. But we should think about it. It doesn't just disappear. The garbage truck picks up your garbage and takes it to a huge hole in the ground. The hole is called a landfill. The problem is people keep making more garbage, and landfills keep filling up! We need to find ways to make less garbage."

"Are we going to have to clean up litter at our party?" asked Jeremy.

Ms. Webster laughed. "No, Jeremy. Don't worry. We'll have fun. In fact, tomorrow we will take a field trip to the supermarket to get ready for the party."

The next day, Ms. Webster's class went to Miller's Food Store. Jeremy was headed for the snack section when Ms. Webster said, "Wait! As we shop today, remember what we have learned about landfills. Let's think carefully about what we buy."

"We need Cruncho Chips!" said Jeremy. "Let's buy the Picnic Pac. Then we'll each get our own bag."

"Wait a minute," said Hector. "If we buy one big bag, we'll have less garbage to throw out, and just as many Cruncho Chips."

"Now that's the Earth Day way to shop!" said Ms. Webster. "Try to buy things that make less garbage. And let's stay away from things we use once and then throw away, like paper cups. We can drink from pop cans or glasses instead!"

Recycle Shopping

When they got back to school, Ms. Webster's class made more plans for their party.

"Let's make posters showing how to help the earth," said Sara. "We can make one about recycling and one about shopping the Earth Day way."

"Splendid!" said Ms. Webster. "And we will also need a poster about saving water. That is very important."

"Saving water? Why do we need to do that? On the globe it looks as if there is lots of water," said Hector.

"Yes, but those are oceans," said Ms. Webster. "They are filled with salt water. It's not good for drinking.

"Fresh water is found in rain, rivers, and lakes. We can't live without it. Neither can animals or plants. That's why it's very important that we don't waste water."

"Great!" said Allison. "The next time my mom wants me to wash dishes, I'll tell her I can't. I have to save water!"

Take a short shower.
Don't let water run when
you brush your teeth.
Fix leaky faucets.

Don't be
a Drip
Save Water!

"That's going a little too far," said Ms. Webster. "But there are easy ways to save water. For example, if you can take a short shower instead of a bath, that will use much less water. And you should not let the water run while you brush your teeth."

Ms. Webster's class thought of other ways to save water. Then Hector went to work on a poster. It said: "DON'T BE A DRIP. SAVE WATER!"

19

"Water isn't the only thing that people, plants, and animals can't live without. We all need air, too," said Ms. Webster. "We don't have to worry about running out of air. But we do need to keep it clean. Factories can make the air dirty. Cars, trucks, and buses make the air dirty too. You can't always see the dirty air, but sometimes you can smell it."

"What can we do to keep the air clean?" asked Sara.

"Well, sometimes you and your parents can ride bikes instead of driving. Or if you know somebody who wants to go where you're going, you can share a car ride. When you use one car instead of two, that makes less air pollution."

"Hector and I ride to school together," said Sara. "We live on the same block. One day his mom drives, and the next day my mom drives."

"I have an idea," said Ms. Webster. "Let's invite all of your parents to school for our Earth Day party! We can show them what we have learned about taking care of the earth. And maybe we will learn that more of you can share rides to school."

The class got busy, making invitations. Then they made decorations from recycled garbage. They used cardboard tubes and empty egg and milk cartons. At last they were ready for Earth Day.

Dear Parents,
    Hope you can come to our Earth Day Party on Friday, April 22.

The party was a big success. First they played games, such as pin the trash on the garbage can. Then they had a picnic. Next the children taught their parents what they had learned about taking care of the earth. Then Ms. Webster had a surprise. "Follow me," she said.

RECYCLE

EARTH
DAY
EVERY
DAY

Everyone followed her to the playground. There was a little tree. Its roots were wrapped in a bundle. "One of the best things we can do for the earth is to plant a tree. Trees give animals a place to live and hide. They give us shade. And they even help clean the air."

Hector's dad dug a hole for the tree, and Hector gave it water.

Soon it was time for the party to end. "Well, Jeremy, did you have fun?" asked Ms. Webster.

"Sure," said Jeremy. "But I was just thinking. If you're supposed to celebrate Earth Day by taking care of the earth, then I think we had Earth Day all week."

Ms. Webster laughed. "That's right, we did. But you know, if we really want to help our planet, we need to celebrate Earth Day every day."

Activities

Our Fine Feathered Friends

Birds are good friends to the earth. They eat bugs that are harmful to plants, they help spread seeds, and they are beautiful! You can be a good friend to birds by giving them food and a place to take a bath!

Pine Cone Bird Feeder

You will need:
—a pine cone
—a piece of string
—2 T peanut butter
—1-1/2 T corn meal

Tie the string around the bottom of the pine cone. Leave enough extra string so you can tie the pine cone to the branch of a tree. Mix the corn meal and peanut butter together. Spread the mixture all over the pine cone, even into the deep parts. After you hang your feeder, watch to see what kinds of birds like peanut butter!

Bath Time!

You will need:
—a plastic or ceramic saucer (the type used under plant containers)
—water

Fill the saucer with about two inches of water. That's all birds need for a good bath. If there are cats in your neighborhood, keep the saucer up high, perhaps on a picnic table. Then watch the fun when birds fly in to take a dip!

Buried Treasure

Some kinds of garbage "break down" when they are buried in dirt. They become part of the earth again. Other kinds of garbage do not. You can do an experiment to prove that this is true.

You will need:

—four ceramic pots
—a trowel
—a piece of styrofoam
—a small plastic baggie
—a piece of lettuce
—a small pile of carrot or apple peels
—dirt

Put some dirt in each pot. Then put the styrofoam in one pot, the baggie in another, the lettuce in the third pot, and the peels in the fourth pot. Cover the items with more dirt. Label each pot for what is buried in it. Sprinkle water on the pots about once a week.

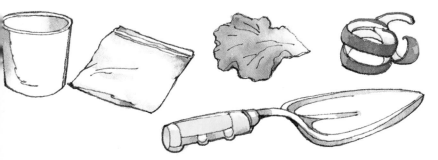

Which of the items do you think will break down in the dirt? Which will stay the same? After one month, dig up the items to see if you can find them. The lettuce and the peels should be almost totally broken down. (They may need a little more time.) But the styrofoam and plastic do not break down. That means they will take up space in landfills for a long, long time. Maybe even 500 years! Which kind of garbage do you think is bad for the earth?

Recycle Your Own Paper!

Do you wonder how old paper is turned into new paper? You can find out for yourself!

You will need:

—2+1/2 single pages from a newspaper
—a thick section of a newspaper
—a blender (and an adult to help you use it!)
—five cups of water
—a big square pan at least 3 inches deep
—a piece of window screen to fit inside the pan
—a measuring cup
—a flat piece of wood the size of the newspaper's front page

1. Tear up the 2+1/2 pages of newspaper into little pieces and put them in the blender. Add five cups of water. Cover the blender and turn it on. Stop when the paper is turned into mush. (This should only take a few seconds.)

2. Pour about one inch of water into the pan. Put the screen in the pan. Pour one cup of the paper mush (called "pulp") onto the screen. Spread the pulp evenly over the screen with your fingers.

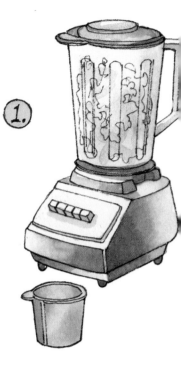

1.

2.

3. Fold section over on screen as shown.

See screen between sections of paper.

3. Open the newspaper section to the middle. Lift the screen up and let the water drain off it for a little while. Put the screen with the pulp on the newspaper. Fold the section over on the screen. Gently flip over the newspaper section so the screen will be on top of the pulp.

4. Put the board on top of the newspaper and press hard to squeeze out the extra water. Open the newspaper and carefully take off the screen. Let the pulp completely dry. (This will take overnight.) Then gently peel it off the newspaper. You have made recycled paper! Try writing on it. You can also change this experiment by adding little pieces of colored construction paper!

(*Ideas from: *50 Simple Things Kids Can Do to Save the Earth,* ©1990 by EarthWorks Press, Berkeley, Ca. Published by Andrews and McMeel. Used with permission.)

3. cont.

...ped over so screen is on top of pulp.

Board on top of paper.